MW00890826

www.mascotbooks.com

Lexi Decker and Her Super Power

For more information, please contact:
Mascot Books
620 Herndon Parkway, Suite 320
Herndon, VA 20170
info@mascotbooks.com

Library of Congress Control Number: 2020923007

CPSIA Code: PRT0121A
ISBN-13: 978-1-64543-882-3

Printed in the United States

For Shayna

With love and a promise to always remind you
that you can do — and be — whatever you decide you can.

And for Lex, a once-shy young boy
who grew up to be a phenomenally kind, positive, confident
force in the world.

When Lexi Decker wanted to ride her bike,
she worried she'd fall down.
"What if I scrape my knee?" she wondered.
"They'd laugh me out of town!"

Out on the golf course one bright morning,
Lexi stood nervously at the first tee.
"What if I swing and I miss?" she thought.
"They're all staring right at me!"

In math class Lexi had an answer,
but she thought she ought to keep mum.
"What if I don't get it right?
For sure they'll think I'm dumb!"

One hot, sunny, summer afternoon
by the diving board at the pool,
Lexi wanted to try a flip, but fretted,
"If it flops, they'll think I'm a fool!"

Once, as she was dressing for a party,
Lexi thought to don a very fancy hat.
But when she looked at herself in the mirror,
she worried what people would think of that.

And then, one day, it hit her.

Lexi finally saw the light!

"Whether I think I can, or I think I can't,

there's a good chance I'm going to be right."

"CAN-fidence is what I need.
Great things come from believing in myself!
I'm going to take all my nervous worries,
and put them high up on the shelf.

I'm going to wear my CAN-fidence cape,
I'll take it everywhere I go.
And regardless of what I'm trying to do,
I will always, always know ...

That if I take my time and a good, deep breath,
if I study and I practice and I try,
then I can do whatever I want —
score a goal, write a poem, bake a pie!

With CAN-fidence, I can ride my bike,
so what if I fall down?!
When I'm riding high, all smiles,
they'll be applauding me in town!

With CAN-fidence on the golf course,
every tee is like the last.
I'll address the ball, and bend my knees,
and give it a good, solid blast!

With CAN-fidence in math class
I can speak up loud and clear.
And whether my answer is wrong or right,
I tried — and that's always something to cheer.

With CAN-fidence on the diving board
when I'm out at the pool,
I'll take three steps, jump up and tuck,
I can somersault! I rule!

With CAN-fidence, getting dressed is a breeze.
I can pick and choose my look.
Colors, patterns, trucks, or flowers,
I don't have to go by the book."

All it took was CAN-fidence,
now Lexi Decker knows,
that she can soar to great, great heights,
and do anything, wherever she goes.

When it comes to making things happen,
Lexi now knows CAN-fidence is key.
Feeling good and proud of yourself
is the only way to be.

About the Author and Illustrator

Amy K. Harris has been a writer and creative thinker all her life. An active, involved, and proud aunt to three now-grown adults by blood, and more than a dozen others by deed, she began authoring children's books when her nieces and nephews started having kids of their own.

Sheila Newman has always been an artist, using her graphic talents to create whimsical drawings, designs, and caricatures in every medium possible ... paper, fabric, canvas, video, and countless others.

Amy and Sheila are "sisters-in-law-ish," and have been working together on family projects since Amy's oldest brother married Sheila's oldest sister. *Lexi Decker and Her Super Power*, their first published book, was created for Sheila's granddaughter and Amy's great-niece, Shayna.